MR PATT...

Stephanie Baudet

Published by Sweet Cherry Publishing Limited
Unit 36, Vulcan House,
Vulcan Road,
Leicester, LE5 3EF
United Kingdom

First published in the UK in 2017
2019 edition

ISBN: 978-1-78226-059-2

Mr Pattacake and the Space Mission

www.sweetcherrypublishing.com

Printed and bound in India
I.IPP001

Pattacake, Pattacake, baker's man,
Bake me a cake as fast as you can;
Pat it and prick it and mark it with P,
Put it in the oven for you and for me.

Pattacake, Pattacake, baker's man,
Bake me a cake as fast as you can;
Roll it up, roll it up;
And throw it in a pan!

Pattacake, Pattacake, baker's man.

Pat-a-cake, Pat-a-cake, baker's man,
Bake me a cake as fast as you can;
Pat it and prick it, and mark it with P,
Put it in the oven for you and for me.

Pat-a-cake, Pat-a-cake, baker's man,
Bake me a cake as fast as you can.
Roll it up, roll it up;
And throw it in a pan!
Pancake, Pancake, baker's man.

MR PATTACAKE
and the
SPACE MISSION

'Yippee!' shouted Mr Pattacake, waving a letter in the air enthusiastically. He began to do the silly dance he always did when he was excited, and his big chef's hat wobbled dangerously.

Treacle, his ginger cat, raised his head and looked at Mr Pattacake. He had just been having a nice nap after breakfast and didn't like to be disturbed.

Nevertheless, he knew that a letter followed by all this excitement could only mean one thing. Mr Pattacake had been offered another cooking job. The thought of all the tasty morsels which always came Treacle's way when Mr Pattacake cooked, made him rise up to a sitting position and take interest.

'Treacle! We're going on a space mission!'

Treacle didn't know what that was. Space? The only space he needed was one to sleep in, preferably in a patch of warm sunlight.

Mr Pattacake always knew what Treacle was thinking. He had been around cats long enough to understand them completely.

'Space!' He pointed upwards and Treacle followed his finger and looked at the kitchen ceiling.

'Outer space,' said Mr Pattacake, impatiently. 'To another planet.' He looked at the letter again. 'The scientists want to study the eating habits of aliens on a planet called *Collywobble* and have asked me to take some Earth food so I can cook them all a meal. And look, they want me to try their food as well.'

Treacle wasn't sure *he* wanted to try any alien food. He yawned and lay down again, losing interest, while Mr Pattacake sat down at the table to make a list of the food he would have to take. He loved making lists.

He wrote down:

Sausages, lamb chops, chips, salad, baked beans, fish, ham, cheese, and lots of vegetables.

He then put: oranges, bananas, pears, plums and strawberries.

Then he went off in his little yellow van to buy the food and pack them all in a box ready to go on board the spaceship.

Treacle insisted on taking his bed, his bowl, some of his dry food and some cat treats.

At last the day of the launch arrived.

Mr Pattacake and Treacle reported to the Space Centre and were given their spacesuits. They were shiny silver and like overalls, that zipped up the front. Mr Pattacake was shown how to use the special toilet on the spacecraft, while Treacle was given a nappy to wear.

What an insult! He sat, looking comical in his little spacesuit with the zip open at the front, shaking his head. This was too much for a cat's dignity. He would definitely NOT wear a nappy as if he were a baby.

'I know you are good at using your litter tray, Treacle,' said Mr Pattacake, trying to reassure him. 'But in space there is no gravity. Things don't fall down.'

But Treacle still sat stubbornly, his ears flattened in annoyance, and his tail swishing. Except there was a problem there, too. There was no hole in the back of his spacesuit, so his poor tail was squashed, with no swishing room. It was all too much!

'Well, if you don't want to come, you'll just have to stay behind,' said Mr Pattacake, changing tactics. 'And you'll miss out on a great adventure, as well as all the tasty food.'

'It's time to get aboard,' said Jim, one of the astronauts. 'Lift-off is in half an hour.'

Finally, Treacle relented, thinking of all the delicious treats he would miss. Mr Pattacake placed the little nappy around the cat's bottom and attached the sticky sides. He had cut a hole for Treacle's tail in both the nappy and the spacesuit.

Treacle waddled about awkwardly, his legs wide apart and very un-catlike. Mr Pattacake stood there watching, trying not to laugh.

Then they both climbed into the tiny cabin and strapped themselves into their seats.

'*Ten... nine... eight...*' the countdown began.

'LIFT-OFF!'

WHOOSH! They were up.

Soon, they left the Earth far behind. Mr Pattacake could just make it out through the spaceship windows – a small blue ball in the sky.

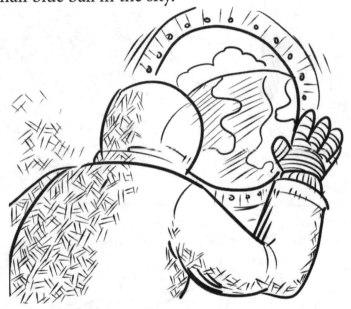

'We're in space, now,' said Captain Starr. 'You can get out of your seats.'

Mr Pattacake and Treacle unclipped their seat belts – and then a strange thing happened. They both floated out of their seats.

Treacle looked scared as he floated past Mr Pattacake, his eyes wide with fear and his tail swishing slowly.

Mr Pattacake did a few slow somersaults. Then he tried to do his silly dance, but it was more difficult than it was on Earth. His legs wouldn't move so quickly, so he just ended up gently bumping against the roof of the cabin like an enormous balloon. His big chef's hat drifted off his head and floated about on its own.

Before they had left home, Treacle had eaten a big breakfast, just in case he didn't like the alien food.

Now, with all the turning upside down, something dreadful happened. He had a nappy on one end, which was fine, but he didn't have anything to cover him on the *other* end.

Sometimes at home, after he had eaten too quickly, he would be sick on the floor and Mr Pattacake had to clean it up.

In space, just as Mr Pattacake said, things do not drop onto the floor. So when Treacle threw up his breakfast, it just floated around, in a little clump, right past Mr Pattacake's nose.

'Ugh! What's that?' he said, trying to back away from it. But the sick just drifted on.

Jim, the astronaut, laughed. 'I think your cat has been sick.'

The sick continued to float about the cabin in a smelly gloop. Jim gave Mr Pattacake a plastic bag and he began chasing the clump of sick around, trying to capture it, but it kept dodging out of the way. It was breaking up into several clumps as well. Mr Pattacake dived after it, holding the bag open, but each time the vomit ducked this way and that, as if enjoying the freedom. At one point it almost drifted into Mr Pattacake's big chef's hat, but he snatched it away just in time.

At last Jim came to the rescue and neatly scooped up the vomit into the bag.

'I think you had better sit in your seat for a while,' he said to Treacle. '*Now* do you see why you have to wear a nappy?'

Treacle looked appalled and sat back in his seat miserably, unable to look anyone in the eye.

Mr Pattacake, Treacle, Jim, Captain Starr, and the scientist spent two long days in the spaceship.

Then at last, through the windows, they saw another planet looming up. It wasn't blue, like Earth, but more yellow and green.

'Collywobble up ahead,' said Captain Starr.

Mr Pattacake's big chef's hat wobbled very gently with both excitement and nervousness. It would have moved much faster if they hadn't still been weightless.

'What are these aliens like?' he asked, hesitantly. He was worried that they wouldn't like Earth food, and would get angry. What if it made them ill?

'We haven't been here before,' said the scientist, who was called Professor Smirk. 'But we have communicated with them. They're a fun crowd, always laughing.'

Mr Pattacake relaxed a little at hearing this. Laughing people were usually happy people.

They strapped themselves into their seats again for the landing, and then Captain Starr opened the doors of the spaceship and put down the ladder.

'You can have the honour of being the first person to step onto the new planet,' he said to Mr Pattacake. 'I've stepped onto many planets in my time. It's your turn now.'

Mr Pattacake, his heart thumping with excitement, went to the door of the spaceship and stood at the top of the ladder looking out at the unfamiliar landscape.

From every direction, aliens were running towards them.

They were strange creatures, yellow and green, with two long arms and round bodies. They all had one large eye in the middle of their foreheads, a nose with very large nostrils, and a large mouth.

...from every direction, all of them were running towards them.

...they were strange creatures, purple and green...with two long, thin arms and legs. They all had...one large eye in the middle of their forehead, a nose...with very large nostrils, and a large mouth.

Their mouths were wide and they were grinning. There was a noise that sounded like a shed full of turkeys.

Mr Pattacake hesitated as the aliens swarmed forward. As he stepped down the ladder and onto the green soil, he realised that the funny noise was actually the aliens laughing.

Mr Pattacake felt his face redden. He had never been laughed at before... well, at least not so loudly and by so many people at once.

Professor Smirk, Jim, and Captain Starr stepped down, to be greeted by further chortles and shrieks, but when Treacle emerged, climbing warily down the ladder and still wearing his nappy, the aliens fell to the ground in mirth.

They chuckled and hooted, holding their sides and rolling around on the ground.

Treacle stood still, his ears flattened. He wished he had never come, what with having to wear a nappy, having his sick floating about the cabin, and now being laughed at by a bunch of aliens. He wished he was back at home. He'd rather be with that mischievous tortoiseshell cat, Naughty Tortie, than here with these rude aliens.

It was horribly humiliating!

Mr Pattacake quickly took off Treacle's nappy, seeing that the cat was getting more embarrassed by the second.

'Don't worry,' he said. 'They do nothing but laugh. I think it's the only way they can show their feelings. They might be really scared of us.'

Nevertheless, Mr Pattacake's big chef's hat was wobbling as fast as it could, and Treacle noticed that he wasn't doing his silly dance. It was just as well. That might be too much for the aliens.

'Right,' said Jim. 'Captain Starr and I are going to collect specimens of soil and rock to take back to Earth, while you, Mr Pattacake, cook up a meal for the aliens. Professor Smirk will be observing the aliens' reactions and studying what they eat, too.'

But when Mr Pattacake fetched the box of food from the spaceship, and opened it, his heart sank. It was all bad.

'Oh dear,' said Jim. 'The fridge must have broken down.'

'But we've only been travelling for two days,' said Mr Pattacake. 'It shouldn't have gone off already.'

Jim shook his head. 'It seemed like two days,' he said. 'But, in actual fact, it was two months in Earth time. Time passes more quickly in space, you see.'

The whole experiment has failed, thought Mr Pattacake, pulling the food out and spreading it on the ground.

The lettuces had caterpillars crawling around in them. The meat and fish were green and wriggling with maggots. The vegetables were squishy and rotten, and the cheese had a layer of thick, furry green mould all over it. The bananas were black, the oranges dried up and the other fruit was all mouldy, too.

Everything smelled disgusting!

Mr Pattacake wrinkled up his nose and Treacle shook his head to try and get rid of the smell.

Mr Pattacake's heart was thumping. What was he going to do? He wondered how the aliens would react if they were angry. Cooking them a meal was the gift they had brought to show that humans were friendly and had come in peace.

As he stood staring at all the rotten food, several aliens came creeping forward, giggling. Their eyes widened when they saw the food and their large nostrils flared, taking in the strong smells coming from the foul food.

There was nothing Mr Pattacake could do. Rotten food like this would make humans very ill indeed so he began to gather it together, shaking his head in defeat.

Suddenly, the aliens rushed forward, making a cackling sound. They almost dived onto the food, picking out the caterpillars from the lettuces and the maggots from the meat and stuffing them into their mouths greedily.

They sucked at the squishy rotten food with big slurping sounds, the juice running down their chins and dripping onto the ground. They ate up the mouldy vegetables, leaving little moustaches of green furry mould on their top lips.

All the while, they chatted and laughed, their mouths open showing the disgusting food swirling inside, sometimes spraying it out as they snorted with laughter. They had terrible table manners.

Finally, when all the food had gone, they all belched loudly, holding their stomachs and hooting with laughter.

Mr Pattacake watched with surprise and a slight queasiness, while Professor Smirk was wildly tapping his observations into his tablet.

Not far away, the astronauts, Jim and Captain Starr, were bending down gathering soil samples while Treacle looked on from the safety of the spaceship steps.

For a while the aliens were quiet, digesting their food, but gradually they gathered together and then indicated that all the humans (and cat) should follow them. Treacle was not sure he wanted to go, as every time the aliens looked at him, they snickered and giggled.

'Come on, Treacle,' said Mr Pattacake. 'You don't want us to leave you on your own, do you?'

Treacle didn't, and he was hungry, too. There would be no leftovers from Mr Pattacake's food, and his own supply of dry food had almost run out, so he reluctantly went along with the crowd.

They passed some farms with livestock in the fields. These were giant fat black slugs as big as cows.

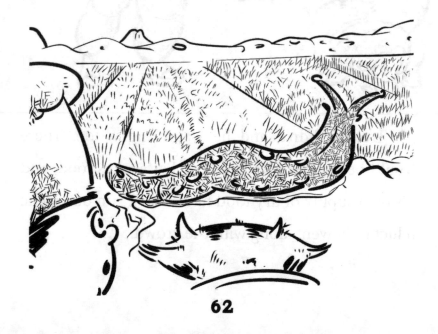

As they slithered along leaving a trail of slime, young aliens followed behind the slugs with shovels, scooping up the slime and putting it into buckets.

There were fields of crops, as well, and orchards with strange, unappetising fruit hanging from the branches of the trees.

Professor Smirk was eager to pick some of the fruit, and the aliens did nothing to stop him, as he reached out and plucked one off a nearby branch. The fruit were greenish brown in colour and smelt like cow dung, with a touch of rotten eggs.

They were soft on the outside, so Professor Smirk quickly put them into his bag and then stared at the brown residue left on his hand. Pulling a face, he took out a handkerchief and wiped it off.

'I think we have been invited to eat a meal with them,' said Mr Pattacake. 'I hope we don't have any of that fruit!'

Soon, they reached a village full of round houses made of mud. They were in a circle around a central area, where many more aliens rushed about, preparing the food.

A fire had been lit, and over it hung a spit, slowly turning a roasting slug. The fire sizzled and spat as the fat dripped off the roasting meat.

Five stools sat in a row, with five wooden boards in front of them. Mr Pattacake thought they were wooden platters waiting for food to be put on them. Aliens clustered round the group and indicated that the humans and Treacle should sit down on the stools. Treacle preferred not to sit on his, which brought another wave of hee-hees and titters from the crowd of aliens.

The roasting slug was taken down from the spit, and one alien was given the task of slicing off the meat and putting it onto the wooden plates. Nearby, another alien held a big pot, and as each plate was filled, he poured a little of the liquid on top. Mr Pattacake had an awful feeling that it was the slime they had collected from the slugs in the field earlier.

The humans were silent as the plates were put in front of them.

'This is the crop we saw,' said Professor Smirk, poking at the peculiar green vegetable with his finger. Instantly, the open pod-like vegetable snapped shut like a venus fly trap.

'Ouch! It bit my finger!' Professor Smirk looked at his finger in surprise, wincing as he rubbed it.

This brought even more loud guffaws from the aliens, but nevertheless, one came to demonstrate how to eat the vegetable so that it didn't bite your tongue. You had to hold it shut as you bit it.

The crowd of aliens fell silent for once, watching in anticipation as their human guests looked at the meal in front of them.

'We have to eat it,' said Jim. 'It would be most rude not to, and they could get very angry.'

'We mustn't be too long, though,' said Captain Starr. 'We need to leave in a couple of hours because Collywobble and Earth will begin moving away from each other very quickly, and then we'll have no way of getting back.'

They were all reluctant to begin eating, so Mr Pattacake, as he was the chef, thought he should try the food first. As there were no knives and forks, he used his bare hands to pick up a piece of slug with hot slime sliding off it. He thought it would be better to close his eyes and imagine it was something else; something like sliced beef and gravy. He took a deep breath and bit off a piece.

Then his eyes snapped open. He wasn't expecting this at all. It was absolutely delicious!

'Mmmm, this is really nice,' he said. Seeing this, Jim, Captain Starr and Professor Smirk all began to eat their slimy slugs, as well. Even Treacle was soon tucking in.

They were very careful to close the venus fly trap vegetables before putting them into their mouths, but it was even more difficult for Treacle to do, and he jumped as one vicious vegetable snapped at his tongue.

When they had finished, they were brought pieces of the foul-smelling fruit. Again, Mr Pattacake was brave enough to be the first to try it. Despite its revolting smell, it tasted like chocolate, with a hint of mint.

The humans clapped and the aliens chuckled and chortled with laughter. Mr Pattacake noticed that Treacle had even made a friend, too. It was a huge black furry CATerpillar, whose face seemed *very* familiar. Where had he seen that face before?

Soon it was time to return to the spaceship. Captain Starr said that if they didn't leave soon they would be trapped here forever as the distance would be too great. Earth and Collywobble would begin moving away from each other at a tremendous rate, making it impossible to get home.

It was then that Mr Pattacake noticed that Treacle was missing, and so was his friend, the CATerpillar.

'We can't go without Treacle,' Mr Pattacake said, pleading with the captain to wait while he went to look for his cat.

Captain Starr just shook his head. 'It's endangering our mission,' he said. 'We cannot risk everyone's life for the sake of a cat. We only have half an hour to lift-off.'

Mr Pattacake didn't know where to start. He tried to communicate with the aliens by making meowing noises, but they just laughed all the more.

Where could that cat and his friend have gone? They could be anywhere on the planet.

He wandered frantically around the area, calling Treacle's name, but there was no reply.

Suddenly, he noticed a little tuft of orange fur stuck to a prickly bush. It was Treacle's fur!

A way ahead was a clump of rocks.

'Treacle!' shouted Mr Pattacake. 'Treacle!' He was getting very worried that the spaceship would go without them. He certainly did not want to stay here forever.

He heard a faint meow.

'Treacle!'

Again came the answer, but there was still no sign of the cat.

Perhaps he was being kept prisoner and couldn't get away.

Then Mr Pattacake had one of his brilliant ideas.

He took a packet of Treacle's treats from his pocket and walked towards the clump of rocks. Then he began leaving a little trail of treats in the opposite direction to the spaceship.

He looked at his watch. Only fifteen minutes before lift-off.

There was a movement by the rocks. Something black crawled out, its head in the air, sniffing. The giant black furry CATerpillar had smelt the treats.

It ventured out further and began gobbling them up.

'Treacle!' called Mr Pattacake again.

A ginger face peered out, nervously scanning the area to see if it was safe. Then Treacle began to run towards the spaceship, streaking across the ground. It was the fastest he had ever run.

But the CATerpillar had many more feet than Treacle. It stopped eating the treats and set off after him, and soon it was gaining on him.

Meanwhile, the aliens came running from the village and joined in the chase. Mr Pattacake realised why Treacle had been kidnapped. It was because he made them laugh so much that they wanted to keep him.

Treacle looked terrified. His ears were flattened and his eyes wide as he ran for his life with the CATerpillar close behind. Mr Pattacake had now remembered who it reminded him of. It was that mischievous tortoiseshell cat, Naughty Tortie, who was always teasing Treacle back home.

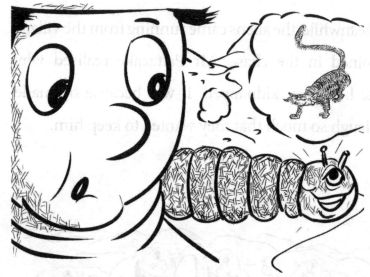

Captain Starr started up the engine of the
spaceship. Mr Pattacake ran forward a few metres
and scooped up the cat just in time.

Together, they leapt aboard, but the aliens kept coming towards them. They surrounded the spaceship and hung onto it.

'We can't lift off,' said Captain Starr. 'You'll have to leave that cat behind, Mr Pattacake.'

But there was no way Mr Pattacake was going to do that. He'd had another idea! He thrust Treacle into Jim's arms and then stood on the steps of the spaceship and did his silly dance.

The aliens stared for a moment and then they began to laugh as never before. Their chuckles and snickers became snorts and guffaws. They held their sides and rolled around on the ground. They laughed and laughed until they were exhausted and couldn't move.

It was then that Mr Pattacake took his chance and sprang inside the spaceship, slamming the door shut on the laughing aliens.

'Lift-off, Captain!' he shouted.

Treacle was so grateful that he even let Mr Pattacake put his nappy on without complaining once.

Mr Pattacake realised that while he was doing the silly dance, his big chef's hat had wobbled right off his head. He would have to buy a new one when they got back to Earth.